Lucy Jane Bledsoe

BASKETBALL

Lucy Jane Bledsoe is the author of four novels, a collection of short fiction, a collection of narrative nonfiction, and six books for kids. She is the recipient of the 2009 Sherwood Anderson Prize for Fiction, the 2009 Arts & Letters Fiction Prize, as well as a California Arts Council Fellowship, a PEN Syndicated Fiction Award, and an American Library Association Stonewall Award. Her stories have been published in dozens of journals, including *Arts & Letters*, *Shenandoah*, *ZYZZYVA*, *Bloom*, *Hot Metal Bridge*, *Terrain*, and *Fiction International*. Her novels have been translated into Japanese, Spanish, and German, and her stories into Dutch and Chinese.

First published by GemmaMedia in 2012.

GemmaMedia
230 Commercial Street
Boston, MA 02109 USA

www.gemmamedia.com

Printed in the United States of America

19   18   17   16   15   3   4   5   6   7

978-1-936846-23-8

Library of Congress Cataloging-in-Publication Data
Bledsoe, Lucy Jane.
   Basketball / Lucy Jane Bledsoe.
        p. cm. -- (Gemma open door)
   ISBN 978-1-936846-23-8
1. Women college students--Fiction. 2. Women baskeball
players--Fiction. 3. Family secrets--Fiction. I. Title.
   PS3552.L418B37 2012
   813'.54--dc23
                                        2012003742

Cover by Night & Day Design

Inspired by the Irish series of books designed for adult literacy, Gemma Open Door Foundation provides fresh stories, new ideas, and essential resources for young people and adults as they embrace the power of reading and the written word.

Brian Bouldrey
North American Series Editor

GEMMA
Open Door

ONE

I'm standing on the free-throw line, sweaty in my uniform, as if the game isn't over. Even the fans are starting to clear out. A few slap my back, move their mouths. They're probably congratulating me on my first Division I game.

I don't even hear them.

All I see is his face. My dad's. A man I met for the first time just now when I shook his hand. He has no idea who I am. Last he heard, like about twenty years ago, Mom wasn't able to have children.

Soon the entire gym will be empty except for me, standing frozen at the free throw line. I finally lope over to the bench and pull on my warm-ups.

I can handle this, right? Sure. No problem.

My gym bag rings. I unzip it, reach for my phone, and check the number. Oh boy. I quickly press IGNORE. It's going to be a long time before I can explain *this* to her.

My mother's message has always been as plain as buckshot. The moment my father broke her heart is the defining moment of her life. Should I choose to ally myself with him in any way, I may as well just kill her.

But tell you what. Let's leave Freud out of it. What are the facts here?

The locker room is empty by now. I strip off my uniform and get under a hot shower. Calm down. Just the facts, right?

I'm a basketball player. Division I recruit for the University of Oregon. Six feet two inches tall.

My mom is shortish, you might say dumpy, and a painter. An *abstract* painter.

Who do you suppose contributed the most genes to me?

Yep, him. And guess what? He happens to also be the father of my two new best friends, Becky and Sarah McCormack, the hotshot twins from Indiana, basketball's mecca.

Like I said, I don't think Freud is going to be helpful here. But the genetics of the situation are sort of interesting. What's coincidence and what's DNA? Our heights are genetic, obviously. But maybe even the highly unlikely fact that we all ended up playing for the University of Oregon has some plausible genetic explanation. After all, Coach Washington recruited all three of us. She's attracted to a particular style of basketball, right? What's funny is that my father spent the last ten years grooming Becky and Sarah for that recruiting moment. Whereas I played in New York—hardly basketball mecca—and for a private school to boot. My mom is supportive of everything I do, and she loves the scholarship, but you couldn't really say her dreams for me ever included athletic competition. So my father's extensive training with the twins might have been superfluous. We all have his ball-playing genes, including a tendency toward a cooperative style and singular focus. All you had to do was feed us and put a roof over our heads.

Mom will like that part. We got what there was to get from Michael. His staying in our lives wouldn't have contributed anything more.

I am, however, on the brink of bringing him into our lives. My life. Mom's life. Michael's life. And maybe most alarmingly, Becky and Sarah's lives. I have to figure out how—or if—to do that.

TWO

Back to the facts. Here's what I know.

Back before she had me, my mom owned a café in Wallop, New Mexico. She was young to have her own business, just thirty-three years old. She did most of the cooking herself, and was famous for her meatloaf, fried chicken, and pies. She'd grown up in Adler Hollow, Arkansas, a town she hated with passion and usually referred to as A-Hole, Arkansas. She didn't like to talk about those early years. Who cares, she'd say, about anyone's painful little mortifications? According to Mom, the human imagination is our only triumph, and we should exercise it to our fullest ability. The rest is reporting, and reporting is always false. Start with the fallibility of facts, she likes to say, and you've started to tell the truth. In any case, I do know that she got pregnant when she was sixteen and had one of those botched abortions, which totally fucked up her uterus. They said she wouldn't be able to have children.

By the time Michael drove his truck through Wallop for the first time, she'd already had shows in a few galleries, one in New York. She was frying chickens and baking blackberry pies, grateful for the hard glare of the sage-scented New Mexican sun, to have escaped Arkansas, to be painting and making something of herself. She once threw a chair across the café when a reviewer wrote that he saw the Missouri River running through every one of her paintings. He meant it as praise, but she thought she'd escaped.

Mom had a lovely house with a big garden. I always feel bad when she describes her eggplants and spinach and tomatoes and raspberry vines, and even worse when she goes on about the flowers she raised, right in the among the vegetables, because now she's stuck in Brooklyn with just two window boxes. Because of me. I'm why she had to leave. New York, she once admitted, is the best place to hide. How do you think that made me feel?

Michael had the fried chicken that came with greens and sweet potatoes, a slice of lemon meringue pie, and four cups of coffee. Mom had given up on men by then. She had her painting, her garden, her café.

As Michael and Mom chatted, he watched the other waitress, Mom's employee, a girl named Merilee. Mom says she wrote Michael off that evening because of the way he watched Merilee's ass. She did notice, though, how easily she and Michael talked. He was a reader, and they liked a lot of the same books.

He slept in his truck that night and came back in the morning for breakfast. He was impressed by the fact that Mom was there again at 7:00 a.m., by how hard she worked and how well she cooked.

The café is still there. Mom and I stopped last summer when we drove cross-country to take me to school. It's kind of a dump now, and that made her sad. She'd put so much work into it. Not to mention, she'd met my father there, although of course she wouldn't admit that the place held any sweet nostalgia for her. It was the work she regretted.

The following week, Michael parked his truck in front again, and Mom thought it was for the food and for ogling Merilee, which it may well have been, but he sat at the counter again, which Mom serviced, and they talked all morning. His route took him through Wallop every week and on the fourth time through, he told Mom that he'd visited two galleries, one in Santa Fe and one in Albuquerque, that showed her paintings. He said, "I like them."

Mom said, "Thanks."

Michael must have been embarrassed by his brevity, because the following week he went into detail about her colors and forms, plowing through his own embarrassment at not knowing the correct art terms because he really did want to tell her. Straightforward, Mom said, direct and honest.

The sex, she told me when I was thirteen, was exceptional.

"Exceptional how?" I asked.

"Exceptionally good." She paused, looked at me, probably considering my age and wondering about the appropriateness of this conversation, and then made the decision she always makes, which is that the truth, the bald truth, is always the most appropriate, and added, "Mind-altering exceptional, life-changing exceptional, flat out the best sex I've ever had." Then she looked momentarily regretful at having said so much, but ended with a shrug and said, "He's your father. You were conceived in that love. You have a right to know."

Even then I knew that "a right to know" meant to know the information she chose to share. It did not mean the right to know him directly.

He quit driving the truck and opened an auto parts shop in Wallop. He said he didn't care that she couldn't have kids. He also didn't care that she didn't believe in marriage. "You should know," Mom told me when I was sixteen, "that love *is* possible. Not likely, but possible. Never enduring. You'll be lucky if you have even a few months of what your father and I had." She paused and then gave me a couple of rare descriptions. "Real tenderness. *Knowing* tenderness."

Then Mom went to New York for a friend's opening and slept with the gallery owner. She says she still doesn't know why. She slept with him *twice*. Her biggest regret in all of life is that she felt compelled to tell Michael about this slip when she returned to Wallop.

He went ape-shit. Completely wall-bonging jealous. He dumped her. Cruelly. He itemized with precise detail every personality flaw in her make-up. He said he didn't know why he'd ever thought he loved her. Within a couple of weeks he was dating Sue, a tall and thin and severely beautiful woman who ran marathons. She wanted children and was pregnant, allegedly accidentally, within months. Michael married her.

Mom sold the café and moved to New York. Not for the gallery owner. She couldn't care less about him. But she couldn't stand witnessing Michael's new life.

Also, Mom, too, was pregnant.

She refused to abort me. She found a doctor who was willing to take the chance and shepherd her through the dangerous pregnancy. We crashed with Sophia, her oldest friend, who had a place in the West Village. For months we lay on a mattress on the floor of Sophia's tiny apartment, Mom holding on to me for all she was worth, me surviving in that damaged uterus. There were days, she said, when she literally squeezed her vagina tight, willed me to stay inside, stay connected to the umbilical cord. To birth me, they sliced open Mom's belly, and they did that a month early. Obviously, I lived. So did Mom. In fact, we thrived.

We spent a full year, the three of us, in Sophia's apartment, all her lesbian friends adoring me and sustaining Mom. She was, once again, through with men, and relished being an honorary lesbian, even if she couldn't will herself to be a real one. Our lives were tentative back then, and Mom likes to say that Sophia's apartment was a second womb, that we were nurtured by her best friend and *her* friends.

Sophia died last year of breast cancer and Mom is pretty much inconsolable. It's the wrong time for me to spring Michael, not to mention my half-sisters, on her.

But I'm getting ahead of myself.

Shortly after I turned one year old, Mom won a Guggenheim. We used the money to get our own apartment. The years flew by as if Michael had never happened. Except, of course, for the oversized girl that is me.

Mom dates two men now. One is married and quite a bit older than she is. He's an arts administrator who says his wife is uninterested in sex and wouldn't mind his having a mistress, although it's best to not let her know. Mom also sees a polyamorous actor, younger than herself, who is lots of fun and severely ADD. He takes her to parties that make her feel young. Sex is reportedly good with both, although very different.

"You are free," Mom said on my eighteenth birthday, "to find your father. Pursue a relationship with him, if that's you want."

Of course by then all the subtexts were crystal clear to me. She didn't need to add: if you do so, you'll destroy me. And: I won't lift an eyebrow to help.

Anyway, I knew my dad was just a story. A good story. I liked Wallop. I liked the fried chicken and pie. I liked his truck. I liked the idea of exceptionally good sex. I didn't need him to be a real person. Mom and I had a very good life.

Which I'm about to shatter.

THREE

Everyone who cares about girls basketball has known about Becky and Sarah McCormack for a long time. They've been legendary since the eighth grade. The big surprise was that they signed with U of O. When I first heard the news last spring, I was devastated by my bad luck. It meant the bench for me. I spent a few long, uncomfortable months thinking of them as my major rivals and even considering going elsewhere. But by the time Mom drove me to Oregon to begin my real life, I'd rallied. Hardy competition was exactly what I needed to shine. I planned on leaving those tall twins in the dust. They'd drive me to be sensational.

This kind of talk always makes Mom a little uncomfortable. Not that she isn't competitive—artists compete all right, but with a veneer of civility. In basketball, you sweat and bleed to get your position on a team, and you never hide the fact that that's what you're doing. You're not only always in competition with your opponents, you're always in competition with your own teammates, vying for starting positions and the most playtime. I love the directness of that. The simplicity. And the honesty.

That's the thing about my mom. She considers starch honesty her trademark. She still thinks she has something to teach me about truth-telling. I've started rolling my eyes when she gets on this track. I tell her that basketball is the most honest game in life. You have a goal: getting as many balls through the hoop as you can. You have grace: moving your body with the greatest degree of precision. You have love: the bonds you form with your teammates are deep.

"I get it, BJ," she said as we drove across the Mojave Desert. "It's like basketball is the metaphor for your life."

"No," I said. "Basketball *is* my life."

Mom helped me move into my dorm room. We went out to dinner with my roommate, another girl on a basketball scholarship, and her parents. Mom left Eugene on the morning of my first practice.

I arrived at the gym a full hour early and skipped the locker room. I was already in my sweats and I wanted to go directly to the court. The lights were still out and the floor had been freshly varnished. The air was cool and dark, with a faint, woody smell. I couldn't believe the expanse of bleachers. The arena was huge. I imagined it full of cheering fans, and my feet turned to ice. I willed them to warm up. I willed myself to rise to this occasion. Me, playing Division I ball. It was my moment. Not my metaphor. My real-time dream come true.

Someone had already rolled in the rack of basketballs, so I grabbed one and bounced it. The echo was hollow and full, a perfect sound. I dribbled to the basket for a simple layup, nothing fancy. Just as I caught the ball falling from the net, I heard the *thunk-thunk-thunk* sound of the lights being switched on.

It was Coach Washington herself. She didn't smile or comment on how early I'd arrived. I knew it was expected that I'd work harder, much harder, than the other girls. I was the wild card among the recruits. Hardly anyone had heard of me. I played for a private school in New York, and while some Division II schools had made me offers, U of O was the only Division I school to recruit me. In fact, Coach Washington hadn't even intended to recruit me. She was visiting a friend in New York, a retired coach, who happened to mention me. I also happened to have a game the next night, and so they went. Coach liked my style of play. She made a point of going back to see me in a few more games. Besides my athletic ability, she thought I had leadership potential. The U of O team had been a bit ragged in the last couple of years, some difficult interpersonal stuff, and a bunch of the girls were graduating. She said it was a good time for a fresh start, that she needed girls who would help unify. I was only a freshman. I knew I was going to have to prove myself.

The McCormack twins were the next players out on the court. I knew them from photos, but they are much more formidable in person. For one thing, they're gorgeous. At six-three, they're an inch taller than me. They have long, thick, dark brown hair which they both wear in messy, swinging ponytails. Big brown eyes. Full, sexy mouths. Every media story comments on how although they're not identical twins, they still look exactly alike. But their personalities, I'd soon learn, are very different. Becky is shyer and still-in-the-closet gay. She always seems a little confused and slow to respond, but these are false appearances that in fact serve her well on the court. In truth, Becky is fierce. Sarah is the front person for the pair. She's funny, loud, and protective of her sister. Even though they aren't identical, they are so obviously bonded that you can practically picture them twisted up together in the womb. After nodding hello to me, they started running their own private drills, complicated and silent and intense. They dropped all twelve of their first shots.

I wonder if they felt their father in me. Unconsciously, of course. I look just like him. I have his gawky nose, green eyes too close together, thin lips, dirty blond hair. Maybe we all somehow sensed our sisterhood. Because from the first minute of the first scrimmage on that first day of practice, we all knew, without discussing anything, that we were going to rule this team as a trio, freshmen or not. I snagged rebound number one, and by the time I looked up, Becky and Sarah had each lane. I shot it to Becky who fired it to Sarah, and we had our two. We stood in a little triangle, briefly clasped six hands over our heads, and that was it.

They roomed together, and I hung out in their room every spare hour. We ate together, studied together, and partied together. They were a blast. I

loved how wholesome they were, sometimes naïve, but open to anything that
came their way. They had a subtle ac-
cent, hokey and broad, and I swear they
smelled like fresh hay. Of course I still
had no idea, at this point, that we were
half-sisters. But I did know all about
their father because they adored him.
I envied the relationship. He texted
them all the time, called almost daily,
always said *I love you*, and advised them
about their game and playing for Coach
Washington. I soon learned that he and
their mother were divorced, and that
he'd gotten custody when they were ten.
They loved their mother, too, of course,
but she was prickly and a workaholic.
She'd remarried soon after the divorce
and they couldn't stand her husband.

They were intrigued by my family, too, and loved hearing about my New York life, which they called glamorous. Once Sarah asked what I knew about my father, and I would have answered if I could have, but suddenly Mom's tales seemed so empty. Hearsay. Just stories.

I especially wanted to tell them about a particular memory, but I was afraid that doing so, telling it out loud, would somehow destroy the dreamlike scene by exposing it to too much light. I didn't want to kill the tender hope in the memory by handling it.

I was ten years old. On a bitter winter morning, at about seven, our doorbell rang. Mom was in the bathroom getting ready for some meeting and she shouted for me to see who was there. Our apartment is on the ground floor of a brownstone, and we can see our front porch if we look out the window farthest from the door. A very tall man stood in the few inches of fresh snow, hands sunk in the pockets of a Carhartt jacket. He wore no hat, blue jeans, and work boots. He struck me as profoundly handsome, like some rare animal spotted in the park. With a hand on the railing, he backed down the six stairs and looked up at our apartment. Some instinct told me to hide, so I let the curtain fall and backed away from the window. But a strong curiosity pulled me forward for another peek. There were snowflakes in his hair.

By now my mother was out of the bathroom and she pushed me aside so she could look, too.

"Oh my fucking God. Jesus fucking Christ." She grabbed my arm way too hard and said, "Stay inside. Do *not* come to the window again, do you hear me?"

By now the doorbell was donging again, and Mom crept silently to the door and pressed her back against it.

"Aren't you going to open it?" I asked.

"Shh," she hissed and held up a threatening finger.

I felt frightened and baffled. Why was she afraid of the handsome man?

The doorbell rang again, and then yet again a couple of minutes later.

Mom canceled her meeting and didn't take me to school, either. In fact, the man came back several more times that day, ringing our doorbell and waiting on the porch. He returned again in the morning, and Mom kept us on house arrest another day. I didn't dare ask any questions. We ate canned soup and dry cereal, whispering and tiptoeing around our apartment, until the third day when the doorbell quit ringing.

Then we carried on with our lives as if nothing untoward had happened. Walking home from the subway on that first afternoon back in the world, I asked, "Was that my father?"

"How silly you are!" my mom sang out. "Of course not."

"Then who was he?"

"No one."

I pretended, even to myself, that I believed her. I never asked about that visitation again, and wondered if it had been a dream.

Sometimes Sophia told me things, and she did so defiantly, right in Mom's presence. Mom would try to shush her, but Sophia argued that I had a right to know what there was to know. She said that shortly after we moved to New York, while Mom was still pregnant with me, my father had come looking for her. He apparently stood outside Sophia's apartment and begged to be let in. He wanted to apologize for being such an asshole, even if he was now married with a kid—Mom and Sophia didn't know about the twins—on the way.

"He was miserable," Sophia said. "Utterly, thoroughly miserable. He knew how badly he'd fucked up and somehow he thought if he could only see your mom, he'd find some kind of redemption for himself."

I couldn't read the look on Mom's face. Full-throated, definitely. Longing, maybe. Pain, maybe. With an overlay of dismay. "Soph. That was a million years ago."

"It's your daughter's history. I'm only—"

"What the hell was I supposed to do? Tell him, come on in! Pat my gigantic belly and tell him to meet his other kid, who—as he well knew—might just kill me in her birth?"

"For fuck sake," Sophia said, laying a hand on mine.

"It's my daughter's history," Mom quoted sarcastically. "She knows how dangerous her birth was."

"I'm not saying you should have done anything differently," Sophia said quietly. "I'm just saying BJ has a right to know he came looking for you."

Mom waved a hand through the air.

Sophia persisted. "There were other times, too. It was like a bear to honey. He never got over you, that much is clear."

"He had his family," Mom said. "He had nothing to offer us. Whose side are you on?"

Sophia shrugged. "It's not about sides. I'm just explaining so she understands."

"Do you understand?" Mom asked me.

"Yes," I lied.

FOUR

We all three got starting positions, Sarah at center and me and Becky as the two forwards. They were excited because their dad was coming from Indiana for the first game. I looked forward to meeting him and hoped that I would be invited for whatever they did after the game, although I felt a little sheepish about that hope. After all, I was just a new friend, even if we were already tight.

Luckily, I didn't see him before the game. I shudder to think how I might have played if I had. It was a dynamite game. We won, 73 to 68. After shaking hands with the other team, I turned to Becky and Sarah, but they looked as though they had closed ranks. They were jumping up and down, waving at their dad in the stands. I headed for the locker room, embarrassed that I felt left out. Someone grabbed my arm and pulled. I turned, and it was Becky.

"Hey. Come meet Dad."

"Now?" I asked.

She laughed. "Yeah, come on." Sarah was already striding across the court toward a tall man standing with his hands deep in his jacket pockets, a gigantic grin on his face.

Would I have known just by the fact that I looked exactly like him? Probably not. Who thinks, oh, I look just like that person? But I saw instantly that he was the man who'd stood on our snowy porch, ringing our doorbell every few hours for two days straight. They introduced him as Michael.

I felt ferociously nauseous. He held out a big hand. It was warm and kind. His nose was long and prominent, like mine. His eyes set close. His hair wispy, dark blond, but going gray.

For a fast moment, I assumed he'd know by touch and sight. My world swirled, and I readied myself for everything to implode. But nothing happened. He was raucous with his two daughters, his *other* two daughters. They joked and then started discussing the game, and I could tell they were going to go through it, play by play. He didn't have a clue about me. I was swamped by a violent wash of jealousy. No one ever had gone through a game with me, knew by a single descriptive word which pass I was talking about, and had something to add about its execution.

They did not ask me to join them for their postgame celebration. Becky and Sarah both gave me hugs and said they'd see me tomorrow at practice, and off they went with Michael to eat and talk and laugh somewhere private.

Which brings me to the current moment. After leaving the locker room, I spend half the night walking around campus, a light drizzle soaking me. I don't care if I get sick, if I lose my scholarship, if I get shipped back to New York.

I don't go to any of my classes the next day, although I do show up for practice. Becky and Sarah are so involved in their father's visit that they don't even notice that I avoid them. Off they go again that evening for another dinner with Michael. He will be flying back home in the morning.

Leaving me with one gargantuan secret.

And a massive decision: when and how.

I guess *if* is also a question. What if I don't tell? I love my friendship with Becky and Sarah just as it is. My father is no longer a dream. But he doesn't have to be a bomb, either.

I feel like that girl at the window, looking out, only now I can look for as long as I like. I don't have to pull back. I can flat-out stare.

This makes me feel powerful, like I'm finally in control of my own life story. I'm the only one who knows, and you know what? I don't think I'll tell.

I've never played better ball. Coach Washington loves what she sees in me, Sarah and Becky. We work. We work hard and we work well. We're a scoring-rebounding machine. We start getting press after just a couple of games.

We also get a lot closer. Sarah is having big issues with her mom, and she quits speaking to her. Becky falls in love with a girl in her dorm and struggles with coming out. Both of them rely heavily on me. I have an amazingly cool mom, in their eyes, and they love hearing how I can—they think—say anything to her. They are also greatly comforted to hear about Sophia and her friends, and how easy it is for me to accept Becky's sexuality. The closer we get, the guiltier I feel about my monstrous secret. And the more keenly aware I become that if I tell it to them, I will betray my mother.

Maybe everyone is hurtling down a path toward betrayal of her mother. It's just part of the extended birth process.

And that's how it happens, like another kind of birth. We're sitting around on a Tuesday night, cracking jokes about how stupid it is that we haven't gone to bed yet since we have weight-training at 6:00 a.m. We're eating the kettle corn Michael sent them. They love kettle corn and swear you can't get the good kind here. I love kettle corn now too. We're laughing about making ourselves sick on it. Maybe the vomit jokes trigger my confession, because it hurls out of me with zero premeditation. I don't plan it. I don't think of a good way to do it. It just happens.

"I gotta tell you guys something," I say.

"What?" they ask in unison, their smiles crushed by the gravity of my tone.

"This is going to sound crazy, so I'll just say it. Michael. Your dad. He's my dad, too."

There should be a word for shocked bewilderment. After a few seconds, Sarah tries to cough out a little laugh, tries to make this into some kind of joke.

I say, "I'm serious. It's true. I can tell you the whole story."

They're staring and they don't look

friendly. I start talking fast. I tell about the café and Merilee. I don't get far though, because Becky interrupts and says, "BJ, this isn't funny."

"It's not supposed to be funny."

They exchange a look. Then Sarah rallies and says, "BJ, we love you. I know it's weird being friends with twins. But you don't have to—"

"No," I say. But I stop because Becky has stood up.

"BJ, don't. What you're doing is kind of sick."

"He doesn't know," I say, hearing the acute desperation in my voice. "My mom had an abortion when she was a teenager. They told her she couldn't have children. That's what Michael thinks. So he wouldn't ever suspect—"

"Stop it," Sarah says. She remains seated, but Becky is at the door saying, "I gotta go to bed."

Sarah then gets up too and pats my knee in her kind, Midwestern way. She just leaves.

The next day at practice they treat me like a mental patient. I can tell they've talked about how to be with me. Their greetings are artificial and too kind. I don't know what to do or say. I've broken our friendship. I've broken everything. We don't eat or study together for the rest of that week, and we also lose our first game. I have never felt so alone in my life. I wish Mom *had* aborted me.

Finally, ten days after my attempt at revelation, I try again. I have to. There's no other way out. I have to convince them. I knock on their dorm room door at about ten o'clock. They're both in bed, studying. I sit in a desk chair and no one says anything for a couple of minutes.

Then I say, "You have to believe me."

"We thought we knew you," Sarah says. "But this is just too weird."

"You need help," Becky says. "You should go see the counselor."

I see everything on their faces. They think I've fabricated this extraordinary story to get inside their twindom. They now see my New York life with my artist mom as lonely and pathetic. I'm unstable. I'm beyond needy.

I see that they're right. I've been delusional, thinking that this friendship with two basketball stars is real. I stand up, burst into tears, and run from their room. That night I pack to go home. But I don't have any money, and when I call my mom, she won't buy me a plane ticket. I don't tell her what's wrong, and she says the first semester is the worst, that I have to hang in. She says it'll get better after the holidays, she promises. She doesn't have a clue, but somehow I'm comforted, just hearing her voice and realizing that she is a real person, not a figment of my imagination.

FIVE

The following weekend is Thanksgiving
and I'm thankful that Sarah and Becky
fly back to Indiana. I have the whole long
weekend to take walks and read and try
to decide what to do. If I tell Mom, she'll
probably let me leave school, at least this
school. After all, she's been running from
Michael her whole life. She'll want me
out of range, too.

But by Sunday morning I've remem-
bered that I'm a basketball player. It's not
the metaphor for my life. It *is* my life.
I'm in the starting lineup on a Division
I team and I've let my personal problems
get in the way. We lost a game that we
shouldn't have lost. I decide to keep my
eye on the ball, literally. Becky and Sarah

are no longer my friends, but they're still my teammates, and I'm grateful for the clarity of that relationship.

I go to the gym on Sunday night. I shoot a hundred free throws. I run suicides all by myself. I practice my three-pointers, a weak part of my game, determined that by junior year I'll have the best three-pointer stats on the team. I run and shoot and pivot and, yeah, sometimes cry, until I feel like all the pain is burned away.

Then I walk back to my dorm room. I hope my roommate isn't back from break yet. I'd like just a couple more hours of solitude.

I open the door and burst into tears all over again. My room has been ransacked. What's going *on*?

Then I look more closely. Ransacked, yes, but benignly ransacked. I find long-stemmed red roses tossed randomly all over my bed and the floor. A plate of chocolate chip cookies sits on my desk. A Danny Granger—my favorite Indiana Pacers player—jersey is laid out on my bed. Three giant bags of kettle corn are propped up on my pillow, and next to them, a note. I unfold the piece of paper and read, "Please come see us asap. Love, Sarah and Becky."

I am so stunned that the obvious doesn't occur to me. Instead I think that they've decided, after discussing it over break, that I need prescriptive kindness. They've developed a plan for rehabilitating me. They'll soften me up with "love," and then once they get back in close, implement some sort of intervention. I wonder if they've talked to Coach Washington.

I tear up the note and begin breaking the rose stems in half. The door opens and Becky and Sarah burst into my room, all arms and legs and words. They're hugging me and crying and saying how sorry they are. I manage to get them off of me and I hold my palms out to keep them at a distance. I don't think I actually say "Back" out loud, but I might.

As Sarah talks, everything starts swirling again.

"We're so sorry, BJ. God, what idiots. We talked to Dad. Dad." She says it three more times, as if she's making room for me in the word. "It's true. Oh, man, he can't even believe it. None of us can. We were going to call you but we decided we wanted to wait until we could be with you in person to talk."

"It's true?" My voice is a whinny. I had begun to think I really had made it up.

"He wanted to come back to school with us. But we wouldn't let him. We wanted to talk to you alone. We've been such assholes. Such huge fucking assholes."

"We just didn't know," says Becky who is quieter and also a bit more defensive. "I mean, we've only known you for a few weeks. So. It just. You know, sounded so absurd."

"It's *scary*," Sarah says.

I feel so confused, and somehow still

angry. I don't want the roses and cookies and kettle corn, though when my eyes fall on Granger's jersey, I realize that I do want that. I don't know if I want Michael or not. I've lived eighteen years without him.

"He said whenever you were ready," Sarah says. "But he really wants to see you."

"We told him you were ours," Becky says. "Not his."

"After all—" Sarah starts, and then maybe thinks better of what she was going to say. Probably something about the eighteen years.

We stay up and talk all night. Literally. Becky says she was gripped by intense jealousy at first. Sarah claims she was thrilled from the first second.

Becky swears that she's thrilled now, too. They both express dismay at how close they came to never knowing the truth. It started because Becky decided to come out to her dad. Sarah sat in for support. Michael was pretty fine with it, although he kept saying she should date men for a while, just to be sure, as if she hadn't already done that in high school. Then Becky mentioned their friend BJ's mother's best friend, Sophia, in New York, and how helpful it had been to hear from BJ about Sophia.

Michael had said, "Sophia? In New York?" Such a thin lead, but he grabbed it.

"Yeah," Becky said, eager to get on with her own story.

"She's BJ's mother's best friend?"

They nod.

"BJ Rogers's mother is Estelle Rogers?"

Sarah claims that she started to believe in this moment, just by the look on Michael's face. She says, "He blanched," and we all laugh at her using that word.

But Becky was still trying to talk about herself, understandably, and so she had continued, "Yeah. She's a famous painter. Anyway—"

"Is BJ adopted?"

By now Sarah was getting an icy feeling in her bowels. Becky was just annoyed that he wasn't listening.

Sarah took Becky's hand, which scared her, and said, "No, she's not adopted."

Michael was actually shaking, they

could see this. He said, "Your teammate BJ Rogers is *Estelle* Rogers's daughter and she's not adopted."

Finally Becky caught up with Sarah and Michael.

Sarah said, "Dad."

Becky said, "Do you know BJ's mom?"

Sarah said, "Estelle wasn't supposed to be able to give birth. She had a bad abortion when she was sixteen. But she did. Give birth. To BJ."

"Oh, shit," Becky said. "We were so mean."

"We didn't believe her," Sarah whispered. Then, louder, "Fucking A. She looks just like you."

Despite our sleepless night, we have an incredible practice the next day. Our

mojo is back. Coach Washington is relieved. She even asks, after practice, trying to sound casual, if we had "resolved"
something over the break.

"I'll say," Sarah says, and we all laugh
way too hard.

Coach looks confused and may-
be even a little left out, but she knows
to leave well enough alone. She's cool
that way. As long as we're at the top of
our game, she doesn't care what gets us
there.

SIX

We tear Cal up that weekend, beating them by sixteen points. Me, Sarah and Becky score fifty-two points between the three of us. From now on, that's how we'll measure our game, by our combined stats. We talk about it that night, how I may have been the one to make that layup but it wouldn't have happened without Becky's pass. How Sarah's rebounds were possible because of Becky's and my blocking.

They let me back in. That fast. We even joke about being triplets, and we practically are, with my birthday just two months ahead of theirs. No one brings Michael up again, but I am well aware that they're waiting for my consent. What they don't know, what I haven't really been able to explain, is how keeping me from Michael has somehow become, over the years, goal number one of my mother's life.

But she would hate what's happening now—everyone but her knowing—even more than my getting to know him.

I borrow money from my roommate, buy a plane ticket, and fly home for the weekend. I don't tell Becky and Sarah I'm doing this until I go to their room on my way to the airport. They nod and hug me. I say, "Don't tell Michael, okay?"

I plan my approach on the plane ride. I will mention that he divorced Sue, the severely beautiful marathon runner, years ago. I will tell her how he has only dated "lightly," as Becky and Sarah put it, devoting himself to them instead. I will definitely tell her how lonely they think he is now. I especially want to point out that it was a couple of decades ago that Michael and Mom had their rupture. Both are different people now. It will be painful for her to hear about what a good father he is, but surely— after the initial stab—that will count in his favor. Most of all, I want to tell her how much I love having sisters.

When she sees me at the door, Mom gasps as if a tragedy has happened, and I realize that for her, it has. I will soon be delivering the details. I imagine her slapping me. Shouting for me to leave the apartment and never come back. I desperately miss Sophia, who would know how to help us negotiate this new territory.

Mom grips my arms too hard. "Honey, what's wrong? Why are you here?"

"I just wanted to come home. I miss you." Both are true. "It's not that big a deal. A six-hour flight. If it were a six-hour drive, I'd come home all the time." Never mind that the short-advance plane fare has put me hundreds of dollars in debt.

Mom wants to go out to some fancy restaurant for dinner, and I can tell that she hopes, unconsciously of course, to ward off whatever painful truth is coming her way with poshness. I insist on ordering out for Chinese food.

I launch even before the food has been delivered.

I say, "You're right, Mom. Basketball *is* a metaphor for life. The intense focus on one thing: an orange ball. And how that—"

"Cut to the chase," she says. "You've come home to tell me something. What is it?"

"And how that intense focus opens you up to all this other stuff. Like love."

"BJ. What."

"I've met my dad."

Her mouth twitches. A bolt of something rocks her chest. But she doesn't look away. She doesn't get up. Quietly, even calmly, she says, "And?"

I'm thrown off, to say the least. You might even say she looks relieved.

"He's Becky and Sarah's dad."

"Yes. I know."

I stand. I pick up a pillow and throw it across the room. A hundred bolts of something shoot through *my* chest. I scream, "You *know*?! You *know*?!"

"I figured it out when we were driving cross-country. You'd mentioned Sarah and Becky before, and of course I noticed their last name, but there are thousands of McCormacks. I guess their being twins diverted my attention. And for some reason I always pictured him having a boy. It never occurred to me until this fall that Becky and Sarah were his daughters. Besides." She pauses and gazes past me, out the window, beyond the bare branches of the tree in front of our apartment, into the soft gray sky. "It's not how I thought he'd show up."

"No. You figured he'd come to *you*. It's always been all about *you*. Your great big love affair five million years ago. And whoops, look what happened, a six-foot two-inch girl. Oh well. Let's just hide her in a Brooklyn closet. It's always been about you. Just you. All about you. Well, guess what. Becky and Sarah are *mine*. For that matter, Michael is *mine*. He's not your lover anymore, but he *is* my father. This has nothing to do with you."

"Well, it sort of does, BJ. I mean, I had a relationship with him. You didn't."

This incenses me. I'm fire-breathing mad. White-heat mad. For my entire life she's kept my father a secret from

me, a man who was living quietly in
Indiana, raising my two half-sisters, a
man who looked for us several times.
While my mom kept us sequestered in
New York where she splattered paint
around and dated dingbats like the old
arts administrator and the young ADD
actor. Because she was too afraid. That's
what I see at last. Her plain old fear. Of
a man she once loved.

Alone. Afraid. Hiding behind the
door and telling me to shush.

I heft my duffel and walk out. I pass
the Chinese food delivery guy who is
coming up our steps. I run to the subway and take the train back to JFK. I
call my sisters and ask for their—Michael's, actually—credit card number,
and they give it to me. I charge the ticket

change fee, and then fly back to Oregon. I keep the blanket over my head the entire flight.

Back in the dorm, I tell Becky and Sarah everything because I'm never going to keep secrets like my mom. For a day or so, they comfort me, and then they gently start suggesting I might have been a bit hard on Mom. She calls every few hours and I refuse to take the calls. Nor am I willing to see Michael. I tell Becky and Sarah to tell him to stay in Indiana.

After a week, I call her. When she picks up, I say, "If you knew, why didn't you tell me?"

"We were driving across the Mojave Desert when I figured it out. You were already entangled with the girls, carrying on about how they were going to drive you to basketball glory. I figured it was destiny."

"The Mojave Desert. Destiny. What are you talking about? This is my *life*."

"I know. I know. I'm sorry. But you have a full scholarship. What were we going to do? Make a U-turn—yes, we were in the *Mojave Desert* and probably didn't even have enough gas or water to turn around anyway—and drive you back to New York? Enroll you in City College?"

"This isn't about you."

"I know that."

It's the first time she's admitted it. That's something.

Then she says, "I figured there was a fifty percent chance no one would ever figure it out, anyway. I mean, how was it going to come up? At least then, when we were driving, you were presenting those girls as enemies."

"No. I *never* thought of them as enemies. Rivals, maybe. Which is completely different. I knew they would be my teammates. I knew I would respect them. You understand *nothing* about basketball."

That shuts her up. She doesn't know what I'm talking about. So I hang up on her.

But something in me starts to shift. I think hard about the look on her face when I told. She had crumbled. In a good way. Like tension letting go. I expected such a different reaction that it has taken me some time to understand. But I think I saw a tinge of hope. Something bright flickered in her eyes. At the time it had made me angry because, yep, it was all about her. But still. I'm not an idiot. I do know that my happiness is pretty much inextricable from hers.

SEVEN

Becky is the one who comes up with the idea. She wants to do it as a surprise. Her face is wild and joyous as she explains how it'll be when they first see each other. She smacks her hands together and says, "Fireworks."

Sarah and I put the kibosh on the surprise part.

"It has to be successful, Beck," Sarah says. "We want it to work."

None of us say what "it working" means.

We go online together and buy the plane tickets, fixing it so that Mom and I will arrive in Indianapolis at the same time. Then they sit with me while I call her.

"Hi, Sweetie," she answers, like everything is normal.

"I'm sitting here with Becky and Sarah," I say.

She remains silent.

"We've just made plans for Christmas. You and I are going to Indiana for a week."

Here's what it feels like: I've opened a door. On my side of that door is a giant vacuum. A little like a black hole. It's sucking my mom through the door. As much as she'd like to say no, she can't even find her voice, let alone words. I smile at the twins, and they silently pump fists in the air.

"Mom?" I say.

"I'm here."

"I really want this."

I think I hear tears. She's nowhere near as tough as I thought she was. She's not even a little bit sophisticated, either. She's pure A-Hole, Arkansas. With some Wallop, New Mexico thrown in. The Missouri River running through.

"What would Sophia say?" I ask. I wait out her silence, seriously wanting an answer. "I mean it. Tell me."

"Sophia would say, 'You big chickenshit. Go say hello to the man already.' She'd also say, 'Do what your daughter asks you to do. She's a hundred times more together than you.'"

"She'd say that?"

"She did say that. On several occasions."

Sarah and Becky call their dad about fifteen times a day before we leave for

Indiana. They tell him to make sure he orders an *organic* turkey. That he gets a grand fir tree, the kind that smells the best. They suggest he weed through their old ornaments, keeping only the best, and that he not, under any circumstances, buy tinsel. He needs to hire someone to clean the house, not just think he can do it himself. They e-mail him a grocery shopping list. They tell their mother that they will spend the entire spring break with her and her husband, but that they won't see her at all over the Christmas break, sorry. Then they leave a day before me, insisting on getting there early to check on Michael's preparations.

I half-expect a no-show. My flight gets in two hours before hers, and I pace the airport. I'm at her gate twenty minutes early. When the plane starts to unload, I count the passengers to distract me from my rocketing anxiety. She doesn't appear to be on the plane. I remind myself that we bought tickets really late and that she's probably seated near the back.

Once again she surprises me, stepping out of the jetway and ambling up the ramp like it was all her idea. She smiles tentatively and looks around, like I might have Michael hiding behind a ticket counter. She doesn't look too frightened. Just a bit startled.

Becky, Sarah and I agreed that an airport meeting would be all wrong, and they arranged to have a car come get us. Michael, reportedly, can hardly stand the idea of not fetching guests at the airport. He says it's rude. And my mom thinks a private ride from the airport is a ridiculous extravagance. But both parents are doing their best to let us manage this holiday.

The shiny black town car does feel incongruous, but that's okay. Mom and I both need the armor. We pull up in front of a plain but large tan house. The driver opens the door for us and then goes around to retrieve our luggage from the trunk. There's a big woodpile, covered with a clear plastic tarp, next to the driveway. An expansive side yard has been paved over and a hoop is attached to the side of the house. About three inches of fresh snow cover the neighborhood, but someone has shoveled and swept the basketball court clean.

Becky and Sarah tumble out the front door. They're wearing warm-ups and Sarah's carrying a basketball. Michael steps out, tall and handsome as ever. My legs practically buckle, but thankfully I see what has to happen now. I take Mom's elbow in my grip, as if I'm her parole officer, and guide her forward. I'm surprised that she doesn't resist. In fact, I feel her presence as soft and aching.

Michael is speechless, his gaze flying back and forth between us. I realize that I can wait. That I want to wait. That by definition they have to come before me.

"Let's shoot a few," I say to Becky and Sarah. They grin.

I let go of my mom, pausing a second,

making sure she's okay. I kiss her cheek and whisper, "I love you."

Michael says, "Estelle."

Mom starts to laugh. I'm mortified. I think she's going into abstract painter mode, diving into her foxhole of absurdity.

But I'm wrong. It's a true laugh. Michael joins her. They actually bend over, Mom holding her stomach and Michael bracing his hands on his knees. They laugh so hard they're in danger of falling over.

We three girls look at each other, realizing that there is so much we don't know.

Sarah tosses me the basketball. Becky says, "Come on." We walk around to the court on the side of the house. I shoot from the sideline and it bounces off the rim. Eecky leaps for the rebound and fires it back to me. I miss four more times, but we repeat this drill until my fifth shot falls soundlessly through the hoop and net.